Apart from being a poet and storyteller, Joanne Cucinello is an entrepreneur, mother, and grandmother. She grew up in Brooklyn, NY, in a musical, artistic family where her vivid imagination was nurtured, and writing stories and poetry became a passion from a young age. Over the years, she channeled those talents into careers as a children's choir director and music composer, small business owner, and caterer. She has self-published four books of poetry and a children's fairy-tale, *Wanda the Wilopent*. She continues to write poetry on the blog, 'I See the Bridge,' since its start in 2007. Joanne hopes her new story, *Lia Paris Sleeps in a Zoo*, will find its way into children's hearts and become a lasting favorite. Joanne currently lives in Port Jefferson, New York, with her family.

Lia Paris Sleeps in a Zoo

Joanne Cucinello

AUSTIN MACAULEY PUBLISHERS™
LONDON • CAMBRIDGE • NEW YORK • SHARJAH

Copyright © Joanne Cucinello (2020)

Ordering Information:
Quantity sales: special discounts are available on quantity purchases by corporations, associations, and others. For details, contact the publisher at the address below.

Publisher's Cataloging-in-Publication data
Cucinello, Joanne
Lia Paris Sleeps in a Zoo

ISBN 9781643782249 (Paperback)
ISBN 9781643782256 (Hardback)
ISBN 9781645367208 (ePub e-book)

Library of Congress Control Number: 2019935635

www.austinmacauley.com/us

First Published (2020)
Austin Macauley Publishers LLC
40 Wall Street, 28th Floor
New York, NY 10005
USA

mail-usa@austinmacauley.com
+1 (646) 5125767

I dedicate this book to my late husband, Al, who was always my biggest fan, and whose love of 'childhood's magic' pushed me to keep writing for children.

I wish to thank my loving granddaughter, Lia Paris, whose early childhood 'zoo' happily led me to pick up my pen and write this story.

"It's not that she's a stubborn little girl," her mama says. "It's just that she wants what she wants. Lia Paris has a mind of her own and she likes to sleep in a zoo!"

Bedtime comes and out come the animals. Oh, she could never bear to leave them upside down or shoved away in closets. They'll start crying and howling... especially Magenta... and then she'll never get to sleep!

6

It all started with Piggy, the little pink pig, Aunt Melinda gave her for a birthday present last year, when she was four. Piggy really liked sleeping tucked under the covers with Lia Paris, all snuggly and warm. It was much better than standing alone on a store shelf. Besides, everyone knows that a soft pink piggy needs lots of love.

A few weeks went by, and one day, her mama saw another piggy at the store. It looked kind of lonely with its big sad eyes, so off it went home to Lia Paris and it was love at first sight for the two little pigs. Soon, they were traveling everywhere with Lia Paris, even in her backpack to hide at nursery school. She made them promise not to squeal and they stayed very quiet. Lia Paris loved her piggies and they helped her fall asleep each night, just knowing she was not alone in her big soft bed.

10

One day, her Nana found a silly stuffed monkey at the thrift shop, who looked like he needed some friends, so she brought him home to Lia Paris. Her soft little piggies giggled with glee when they saw him and thought he looked like a movie star! Little did they know, he would try to tickle them all night and run around under the covers. After all... he was a silly monkey!

Months went by and soon it was spring. Lia Paris loved the springtime, and she promised her three little friends a nice picnic when the first warm day came along.

14

Oh, they were a happy little crew, just the three of them and their dear Lia Paris. But that wouldn't last for long.

Her daddy came home after work one day with two fluffy toy puppies and Uncle Adam thought she'd like a white teddy... and perhaps a green teddy too. That was a super day, full of surprises.

Lia Paris was so delighted, until bedtime came and she looked at her bed. What to do... what to do! How would they all fit on the pillow next to her?

Oh well! she thought. *We'll be a little squashed, but that's alright; at least my monkey will have some other animals to play tricks on.*

It seemed that her little piggies were getting all worn out with Monkey's shenanigans! They'd be happy to get a break! Besides, some nights her little pink Piggy secretly wished things were the way they used to be, when she was the only one in Lia Paris's bed. But she was never forgotten and always wound up in the little girl's arms when morning came.

Spring turned into summer and now it was time to fill the kiddy pool. Water is not a safe place for small stuffed animals, so Lia Paris had to leave them inside while she and her little sister, Simone, splashed around in the pool. She propped her animals up on the windowsill so they could watch and they all felt happy... and dry.

One summer night, her grandpa stopped by and tucked under his arms were two silky kittens for her collection, which by now was starting to look like a zoo on Lia Paris's bed. At least that was what Mama said when her little girl ran in the house to introduce the new kittens to the others.

"Soon, there won't be any more room on that bed for YOU, little Miss Zookeeper!" she said.

"Don't worry, Mama, I'll make room." And she did that night... when she fell off the bed!

"See! What did I tell you?" Mama said as she picked up her crying child and sat her on her lap. "Now some of these animals have got to go on the shelf!"

"But Mama, they'll be sad."

"No, they won't, dear. They'll be just fine."

BAAAAA! sobbed Lia Paris, clutching her furry friends as tight as she could.

"They're scared of the dark, Mama. They'll be squealing, and barking, and meowing all night long. You won't hear them... but I will and my ears will hurt and," she sniffled, "my monkey will make-believe he's a big gorilla again and bang on the wall and... *sniffle*... I'll never get any sleep... and... and... I won't be able to get up for school" she whimpered, as she rolled her big brown eyes.

"Alright... alright, but this is the last time. If you fall off the bed again, things are going to change in this zoo! Is that a deal?"

"Oh yes, Mama. You're the best! I love you."

She gave her mama a great big hug and crawled into bed, fixing her little friends on the fluffy pillow next to her. Counting them one by one, making sure there were nine, she let out a great big yawn, and fell fast asleep.

28

The beautiful moon was shining softly through the bedroom window that night. All was peaceful and quiet, when suddenly there was a thump on the floor, and then another, and another... eight bouncy thumps to be exact! The sounds made Lia Paris toss and turn in her bed. Then she opened her eyes and looked around. She was all alone on her bed, except for her little pink Piggy. There was just enough moonlight shining in her room so she could see. Rubbing her eyes, Lia Paris looked at the floor and all around the room were the rest of the animals in her zoo. She got out of bed and scooped them all up in her arms. She looked at her bed and little Piggy just lying there on her pillow. Then she looked at all the stuffed animals piled in her arms. Her bed looked so comfortable now with just Piggy there, and so Lia Paris made a very big decision that night. She put all her animals on her soft window seat and covered them with an extra blanket from the foot of her bed.

Hmm, she thought, *they all look pretty happy here, don't they, Piggy?*

Just then, Mama opened the door and said, "What was all that noise I heard?"

"Oh, I think it was getting too crowded on my pillow and the animals fell off my bed."

"Really?" asked Mama. "Well, my little zookeeper, maybe now you'll finally get a good night's sleep... and so will I!"

Lia Paris jumped into bed and began to spread her arms out onto her soft, fluffy pillows, and stretch her legs in any direction she wanted. Mama fluffed up her comforter and tucked her and Piggy in with a good night kiss.

Wow! she thought. *This is much more comfortable, isn't it,* Piggy? Lia Paris looked down at her little pig and noticed that somehow there was a smile on Piggy's pink face that never was there before and they both took a big deep breath, closed their eyes... and for the first time in a long, long while, fell fast... fast asleep.

The End.

CPSIA information can be obtained
at www.ICGtesting.com
Printed in the USA
BVHW021034270120
570603BV00015B/172